PUFFIN B

The Last Gold Diggers

Roo lives with Harry Horse and Mandy at Christmas Hill Farm. She has turned down several film offers since the publication of *The Last Polar Bears*, preferring instead to concentrate on rabbits. It is her ambition to own one eventually. She is currently working on her first book, provisionally entitled *The Bad Rabbits*.

Harry has written and illustrated several children's books, including *The Ogopogo – My Journey with the Loch Ness Monster*, which won the Scottish Arts Council Writers' Award. He is well known as a political cartoonist and has produced cartoons for the *New Yorker*, the *Guardian* and *Scotland on Sunday*. Unusually, rabbits do not play a large part in his life.

Another book by Harry Horse

THE LAST POLAR BEARS

Harry Horse
The Last
Gold Diggers

Being, as it were, an
Account of a Small
Dog's Adventures
Down Under

PUFFIN BOOKS

PUFFIN BOOKS

Published by the Penguin Group
Penguin Books Ltd, 27 Wrights Lane, London W8 5TZ, England
Penguin Putnam Inc., 375 Hudson Street, New York, New York 10014, USA
Penguin Books Australia Ltd, Ringwood, Victoria, Australia
Penguin Books Canada Ltd, 10 Alcorn Avenue, Toronto, Ontario, Canada M4V 3B2
Penguin Books (NZ) Ltd, 182–190 Wairau Road, Auckland 10, New Zealand

Penguin Books Ltd, Registered Offices: Harmondsworth, Middlesex, England

First published 1998
3 5 7 9 10 8 6 4

Filmset in 13/15 American Typewriter and 12/15 Bookman

Made and printed in England by Clays Ltd, St Ives plc

British Library Cataloguing in Publication Data
A CIP catalogue record for this book is available from the British Library

ISBN 0–140–37676–3

For Mandy and Roo

25 November

My dear Child,

I am writing to let you know that Roo and I are safe. By the time you read this letter, we will be on a plane to Australia.

I am sorry that we couldn't say goodbye to you, but I had to leave the house in the middle of the night as I knew that your mother and father were against the idea of me going on this trip at all. When I first told them of my intention to go to Australia, anyone would have thought I was going to the other side of the world, the fuss they made. I am afraid I had to creep out of the house like a mouse, being careful not to wake any of you. I may be seventy-nine, but I can still creep out of a house without waking anyone. Roo nearly gave the game away though. She started barking at a reflection of herself in the hallway mirror. I had to zip her up in the golf bag to keep the noise down.

I am going to Australia to find my brother, your Great-uncle Vincent. He's the oldest of my five brothers. When he was seventeen, he stowed away aboard a ship and went to Australia.

We were terribly upset when Vincent ran away, and my father called the Home Office, but there was nothing to be done. All he left us was a note:

Cheerio (it said),

Gone to get gold in Australia. When I find some I will bring it back. Regards,
Vincent

For many months we heard no other word from him, and then one Christmas he sent us a parcel containing unusual things he had found in Australia (an ostrich egg, a boomerang, a dried-up witchetty grub and some quills from a spiny anteater), with a letter explaining that he was now a gold miner and had his own mine in Dust Valley. Although he hadn't found any gold, his prospects looked good. He wrote to us every month, no matter where he was, until over the years I had collected hundreds of postcards. He told us how he had lived with Aborigines in a cave, how he had ridden a donkey all the way across a terrible desert and had ended up carrying it most of the way on his back and how he had fought with a shark off the Great Barrier Reef. But he had never found any gold.

Then, suddenly, the postcards stopped arriving. Had something terrible happened to him?

Here is one of the last cards I received from your Great-uncle Vincent. It shows a picture of a kangaroo in a hat, and on the bottom it says 'G'day, Mate' in large friendly letters.

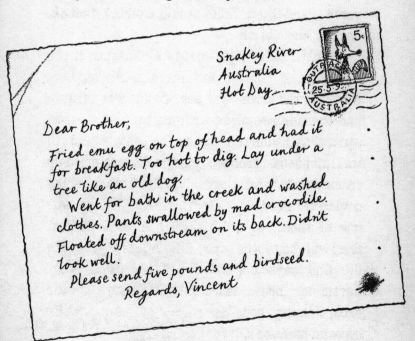

Snakey River
Australia
Hot Day

Dear Brother,

Fried emu egg on top of head and had it for breakfast. Too hot to dig. Lay under a tree like an old dog.

Went for bath in the creek and washed clothes. Pants swallowed by mad crocodile. Floated off downstream on its back. Didn't look well.

Please send five pounds and birdseed.

Regards, Vincent

It worried me to read this postcard, Child. My brother is eighty-four. He shouldn't be fighting crocodiles at his age. I decided then that I would go to Australia and bring him home. I knew it would not be easy to find him. Australia is a big place, and most of it is wild bush country and unexplored regions. I hoped that I was not too late to find him.

I went to the library and read all I could about Australia — where it is, what it looks like, and what type of animals live there. I couldn't find much about Dust Valley and I couldn't find the Snakey River at all.

I booked a flight on Quality Airlines, as it was the cheapest I could find and also the only one that allowed dogs. You see, Child, I'm afraid I had to bring Roo along with me to Australia. Of course the ideal would be a proper tracker dog, but I couldn't afford one of those, so Roo will have to do. She says her particular breed is exceptionally good on sand because it

The only books I could find in the library on Australia.

4

has special paws that stop it
slipping on the steep
bits. I'm sure that
at some point in
the expedition
this will prove
to be useful.

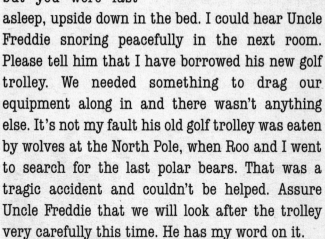

We left the
house while you
lay sleeping. I did
look in on you, Child,
but you were fast
asleep, upside down in the bed. I could hear Uncle
Freddie snoring peacefully in the next room.
Please tell him that I have borrowed his new golf
trolley. We needed something to drag our
equipment along in and there wasn't anything
else. It's not my fault his old golf trolley was eaten
by wolves at the North Pole, when Roo and I went
to search for the last polar bears. That was a
tragic accident and couldn't be helped. Assure
Uncle Freddie that we will look after the trolley
very carefully this time. He has my word on it.

Don't worry about us, Child. We have my old
scout's compass. We won't get lost.

Roo has told me that you can look after her
bone. It is behind the sofa, underneath her

blanket. I have brought her basket with us, so do not look for it.

Send my love to your mother, and tell her that I'm sorry, but I had to go. We will find Uncle Vincent and bring him home. I miss him.

with love,
Grandfather

Quality Airlines
We Only Fly The Best

NON-STOP QUALITY FLIGHTS TO AUSTRALIA

ALL WELCOME. BRING SANDWICHES. FREE TEA FOR LIMITED PERIOD.

DORKING   KWINKWAT   SIDNEY

26 November
On board the *Unflappable*

Dear Child,

We are flying, as I write this letter to you, high above the Atlantic Ocean. The pilot has just announced over the tannoy that we are flying at a thousand feet, which must be very high, although I am sure that I saw the top of a tree out of my window a little while ago. Still, I am sure that we are in safe hands. The captain is a very helpful chap and even came out of the cockpit to serve us tea, because the air stewardess had a touch of air-sickness and wasn't feeling very well.

Roo has been a real nuisance, I'm afraid. I am sure that dogs are very able at all sorts of things, but flying is not

7

one of them. She is too fidgety and won't sit back and enjoy the sensation of being in the air. First of all she stared at the people sitting behind us, standing up in her seat, with her paws over the head-rest, watching them eat their sandwiches. Then she became very restless and began wandering up

and down the aisle of the plane, sniffing people's feet.

Later she started to roam the plane with three little children, crawling under seats and playing hide-and-seek. I am afraid she thinks we are in a bus, and I have given up trying to explain why she can't see any houses out of the window.

In the end I'm afraid I had to give her a good telling-off. She slunk away and sat beneath a woman in the third row — later she sat in her lap and ate most of her dinner. When I tried to coax her back, she became very silly and pretended not to hear my calls and instead went off and chased a child's ball she had found up and down the aisle of the plane.

Drat! Roo did this!

The air stewardess, Brenda, got very annoyed and said that Roo must be kept on a lead always, particularly when the plane was taking off or landing. Brenda then demonstrated the safety procedure for us, inflating an old orange lifejacket, which she put on me! Then she threw a blanket over us both and told us to go to sleep.

I must say that this plane is not quite what I expected, though I knew that things were a bit on the cheap side when we were asked to walk a couple of miles to get on the wretched thing. The plane was standing behind an old disused shed by the runway. It sagged in the middle. As we were boarding the plane up an old ladder, I noticed a dirty-looking fellow shovelling coal into a bucket.

The interior of the plane is not what I expected either. For a start, there is not a great deal of room. The people in the row of seats next to ours have to keep their suitcases on their laps, as there is no room in the baggage compartments. The seats are not comfortable either.

And this!

Mine is an old armchair nailed to the floor, and Roo's is the driver's seat out of an old car. The windows are not the normal sort that you would expect to see in a plane – the one we are seated next to looks as if it came out of a potting shed. It is also very hard to go to sleep. The plane makes a fearful sound, more like an old steam train than a plane, and sometimes it shakes violently. This afternoon one of the wings began to wobble, until the pilot came and tightened up some bolts under my feet and told me to keep an eye on them.

Roo is worried about being upside down in Australia. Tried to explain to her that, although Australia is beneath us, the people who live there do not live on their heads. She said her grandfather went there to be a sheepdog on a farm, and he got used to walking upside down, so much so, in fact, that he even preferred it to being the right way up.

I tried to get to sleep, but Roo kept fidgeting about so much it was impossible. She said she felt hot and wanted to go outside for a bit. I tried to explain that we were high, high up in the sky, but she said maybe she could just have a little walk up and down the wing of the plane. No one would mind. I told her that if she stood on the wing she would fall off and I would mind.

Instead, I showed her clouds to take her mind off being in the plane, and we saw ones shaped like huge islands, with mountains and pink lakes. Some were shaped like animals, and Roo said she saw one shaped like a small sheep in a field of snow.

The sun was going down on our side of the world and we were flying around to the other side, chasing after it, to see it rise above Australia. The clouds swallowed us up and led us into the night. We settled down for the evening. Then Brenda gave everyone a mug of weak tea, turned the lights off and told us to watch the film.

The film was called *The Ghost of Flight Thirteen* and was all about a plane that gets haunted by the ghost of a crazed pilot who still wants to fly. The special effects were marvellous, particularly the bit where the plane flies upside down doing loop-the-loops. Most of the passengers jump out of the plane on parachutes, with the exception of Rock Hunter, the hero, who ends up fighting with the ghost on the wing, before crawling back into the plane and saving it from crashing

Roo is in and out of here
—the whole time!!

into a mountain. Then he gets married to the air stewardess and flies away with her in a hot-air balloon. I fell asleep just as the balloon was attacked by ducks.

I thought it a strange choice of film to show on a plane, but Roo said that it was one of the best films she had ever seen, and wished we were in a plane. I did not feel like explaining again.

After the film Brenda brought us some more tea, but said that milk, sugar and biscuits were now off the menu until further notice. Some of the passengers became quite angry at this and demanded an explanation. Eventually the pilot came out and told them, quite rudely, to keep the noise down.

It is very cold, Child.

Several of the passengers are wearing all their holiday clothes at the same time. Fortunately I brought most of my winter clothes with me.

Too cold to write any more, as it is difficult in these mittens.

Brenda has just walked past with another bucket of coal. I have never seen coal on a plane before. Perhaps the pilot has a fireplace in his cockpit.

Will write more when we land in Sydney, Australia.

with all my love,
Your Grandfather

28 November
On board the *Unflyable*

Dear Child,

Roo keeps asking when we will land in Australia,
and I have to keep telling her not yet but soon. She
is very bored with the flight and wanders up and
down the aisle of the plane looking for mice. I have
told her that there are no mice on planes, but she
is insistent that she has heard them scratching.

When the pilot came down to our end of the
plane to have a cup of tea, Roo asked him if she
could have a go at steering the plane. The pilot
said no. It is true that once Roo did steer a ship.
It is also true that we came to no real harm that
time, but the idea of her steering a plane is a

14

dreadful one. I was relieved when the pilot refused, and I thanked him for being so sensible. He explained that the plane was only ever flown by him, Brenda, and occasionally his pet monkey, Noddy. Nobody else.

The journey is taking a long time. I was told at the airport that this flight normally took twenty-four hours, but we have been flying for a few days now. I have used the time to read more about Australia so that we will be prepared when we enter the outback. Some extremely interesting creatures live there. I would particularly like to see the duck-billed platypus, and perhaps the wombat, and of course I look forward to seeing the kangaroos. I have told Roo about all these creatures, but I decided not to mention some of the more dangerous animals found in Australia.

Hopefully we won't run into the funnel-web spider, whose bite is fatal, I am told, and we will try not to step on the tiger snake, the most poisonous snake in the world. But if we do we will be as polite as possible, then run away as fast as we can.

Using a map, with all the telegrams and postcards that Uncle Vincent has sent over the years, I began to trace his last route, in search of gold in Dust Valley. He had paddled up the Snakey

River in a canoe, then trekked by camel to the camp at Gold Town, and finally walked on foot, with his donkey, through Dust Valley.

Here is one of the last cards he sent:

Dust Valley

Dear Brother,

Still not a sniff of gold in this blasted desert. Got so hot yesterday had to crawl into a hole to shelter from the sun. Snake following me for the last week. Tried to crawl into hole with me. Had to tie it in knot. Donkey sick. Eaten poisonous bush and a pair of good socks. Had to carry him and all the luggage on my back.

Had a touch of gold fever last night. Thought that the donkey was a big block of the stuff, and tried to put him in rucksack. Still sulking about it this morning.

Please send five pounds.

Regards,

Vincent

This worried me. Your Uncle Vincent shouldn't be fighting snakes at his age, let alone having to carry sick donkeys around. When I find him I will bring him back to England so that he can spend

16

the rest of his life in comfort.

Finished planning our route and explained to Roo her role in our mission. It is my intention to harness her to the golf trolley so that she can drag it up the steep bits. We will begin our expedition by advancing up the Snakey River and heading for Gold Town. I think we may even hire a canoe. I have been in the rowing boats at the park and I'm sure that it can't be too different in a canoe. I know I will have to keep Roo on a lead in case she jumps out.

Do not worry about us, Child. I am sure that we will land safely in Australia in no time.

Take care,

with love from your Grandfather

P.S. Hurrah! The pilot has just announced that we are only several hours away from Sydney Airport. Loud cheer from all the passengers, and some hissing and booing as well. Cannot wait to get off this plane!

29 November
On board the *Unforgettable*
Kwinkwat Airport

Dear Child,

We have not landed in Australia. This is because the winds were too strong and consequently we were blown backwards most of the night. Brenda gave us breakfast and then we landed on a small coral island to stock up with more coal, bread rolls and milk.

We all crammed to the window aisles to see where we had landed, and some of the passengers began to drag their suitcases out and change into their swimming costumes when they saw what lay outside.

It looked a beautiful place, with a pure white coral beach shaded by swaying palm trees and a charming blue bay. Some of the passengers asked where they could buy souvenirs and take tea and cake, but Brenda was insistent that NOBODY should get off the plane. She said it was best for our safety, unless we wanted to help load coal. There was a mad charge for the exit as all the passengers squeezed out of the plane and trooped into the coalshed. It was wonderful to stretch, and Roo ran round and round in circles on the runway until Brenda told her off.

I now find out that this plane is the only steam-powered plane in the whole world. The stoker has to work almost non-stop to keep the boiler fed with coal, and although the plane does fly, the weight of the coal needed to keep it going means that we can't go very fast.

Brenda and the pilot watched us load on the extra coal. The first time we took off we had to return after five minutes, as we had left an old lady behind in the coalshed. She was very upset, and Brenda had to give her a complete dusting-down.

Our steam-powered plane managed to get 'above the wind', as the pilot termed it, before we had the first of many problems. Apparently, the pilot explained, some of us had put on weight since the plane left England, and therefore we had to jettison some of the luggage to make the load lighter. Fortunately Brenda didn't pull my stuff

out of the hold, but there were some very angry passengers who watched as she threw their suitcases, hampers and holdalls out of the emergency exit into the sea below.

Can't write much now, Child, as it is very hard to see. The boiler is playing up, and the cabin is very smoky. Also Brenda is smoking a cigar, which I thought wasn't allowed. The stoker came in and broke up a couple of the seats with a hatchet.

The pilot has announced that we will be landing in Sydney soon, but as he said the same thing last night, there wasn't such a loud cheer this time. Roo is very excited. I told her all about the harbour, the bridge and the beautiful opera house that Sydney is most famous for.

Will write soon.

with love Grandfather

30 November
Sidney, Australia

Dear Child,

We have landed in the wrong Sydney. This is not the famous Sydney Harbour, the jewel in the Australian crown. This is the wrong Sydney. Complained to Brenda and she said it was clearly marked in the brochure as Sidney.

This Sidney does not have an opera house, or a harbour. All it has is a small, rusty bridge and a corrugated-iron shed. A group of small animals met us on the runway and asked to carry our bags. I gave my overnight bag to a sort of racoon-type creature, and he ran off into the bush with it.

The man in the tourist information hut was very helpful, but as it was the Sidney Annual

Sheep Fair all the hostels and hotels were full up, and the only accommodation available was a room in a place called Woolly Tree Farm.

We are going to catch a bus to our lodgings. I will send you more news when I have some.

Please tell your mother that I am quite well. I am checking my boots for spiders regularly.

with my love,
Grandfather.

1 December
Woolly Tree Farm
Near the wrong Sidney

Dear Child,

Woolly Tree Farm is not what we expected. It looks like a big shed. When we arrived, a small man came out and looked us over. He took great interest in Roo and insisted on inspecting her teeth, then he offered me five pounds for her on the spot. I explained firmly that my tracker dog was not for sale.

When I told him that we intended to make an expedition into the outback to find my long-lost brother, he laughed and said he hadn't taken me for a bushwhacker. Taken aback by his rudeness, I informed him that I had no intention of whacking any bushes, had never done so, and did not intend to. He explained that a bushwhacker was a man who lived in the bush. I told him that I didn't...

After he had shown us our room, a sort of bunkhouse where the sheep-shearers stay, with an old rickety camp-bed and a bucket, he asked me to help him feed the sheep. Of course I humoured him, feeling that a refusal might

offend. Most of the time I hadn't a clue what he
was talking about, though I learned that his name
was Shorty Watkins and he had a thousand sheep
and no sheepdog.

Shorty drove us out to a big field that had no hedges or fences, so wasn't really a field as we would know one. For miles in each direction there were sheep grazing on the tough grass. Roo ran around barking at the sheep, which I thought ordinary dogs weren't supposed to do as it worries the sheep, but Shorty seemed very pleased and upped the price to six pounds. I did not bother to answer. After we had run the sheep round in a big circle, we retired back to the farmyard and there Shorty cooked us a meal in a large pot.

As the sun began to set on the red hills, Shorty took out an old harmonica and began to play a tune. It was a sad tune and some of the sheep started bleating in harmony. Roo became rather sentimental and started telling a story about her grandfather, a dog that worked for a gunfighter, a story that impressed Shorty but annoyed me.

Apparently in between being a pirate's dog, a doctor, a lifeguard and an actor, Roo's grandfather had stowed away on a ship to America and had ended up belonging to a gunfighter called One Eyed Jack. Roo explained that this fellow could shoot a hole clean through a penny thrown in the air with a single shot from his pistol. The targets got smaller and smaller, and soon One Eye, or whatever his name was, was shooting at a flea holding a grain of rice. Then it got rather silly. Something about Roo's grandfather and a game of cards, and how he used to walk round the table looking at the cards of the other players, which sounded like cheating to me, spelling out to his master the cards that they were holding by using a tail-wagging code. A terrible argument began when this despicable practice was found out, and in the shoot-out that followed, One Eye shot all the buttons off his opponents' coats, even their trouser buttons, so that their trousers fell down.

Shorty roared with laughter at this bit and begged Roo to tell him it again. This she did, twice. Then she told him how her grandfather had been captured by passing Apache Indians and had lived with them in the chief's tepee.

Before she could begin the bit about the dancing with wolves, which I have heard before and still don't believe, I stood up and announced that it was time for bed. Roo came along reluctantly, and we left Shorty and the sheep by the campfire. I have made Roo's basket comfortable, with her eiderdown draped inside, but she refuses to use it, saying there's probably a snake in it, and although I have demonstrated with the aid of a golf club that there is no snake curled in the basket, waiting to pounce on her, she will not lie in it.

When we went on our journey to the North Pole she didn't sleep in her basket either, and I had to carry the wretched thing all over the place, even up mountains. I won't carry the basket all the way across Australia if she is not going to use it. Told her so, and all she said was that she liked to have it around for sentimental reasons as it reminded her of home. Sometimes she makes me very cross.

Roo remains in my bed.

with love Grandfather

Roo helping to break wood up

P.S. Shorty is going to post this letter for me in Sidney. Please could you ask your mother to send some shorts as I forgot to pack any, and it is really hot here in Australia. Our new address will be The Mailing Station, Gold Town.

Dear Child,

Unable to begin our journey as the weather is too hot. So hot that Roo asked to sit in the fridge. This is dangerous and I wouldn't allow it, because you can't breathe in a fridge and you would certainly die, so I draped her in a wet towel instead and she lay panting under an old orange box on the veranda.

I went and lay on the bed and tried to rest, but I couldn't sleep. A bell bird sat outside my window and chimed every half-hour.

We cannot travel in heat like this.

This afternoon I tried again to explain to Roo her role in the tracking of Uncle Vincent. I showed her his baby bonnet, the only item of his clothing I could find in the attic, and asked her to sniff it so that she could get Uncle Vincent's scent. I have seen rescue dogs on television do this. It helps give the dog a clear picture of the person they are trying to find.

Roo snuffled and sniffed at the bonnet for a long time. She chewed on it and even shook it fiercely. Suddenly she announced that she now had a clear picture of him, almost as if he was standing in front of her. Excited, I begged her to describe what she could see. He was small, she said, walked on all fours and dribbled.

I wish now I had brought a real tracker dog.

Have decided we will advance up the Snakey River to Gold Town in a rowing boat. Shorty said he didn't think that was a good idea. He told me there are all sorts of nasty things in the creek. He said his father once sailed up the creek and when he got back his hair was pure white and for a whole week all he could do was sit in the woodshed and gibber. Apparently he had seen something huge with big eyes and big teeth looking at him.

We will now walk alongside the Snakey River. Explained my new plan to Shorty and again he sighed and shook his head. It was too dangerous to wander into the bush on foot for part-timers like us, he said. Then he stumped off behind the sheep-shed and returned a moment later leading a large camel on a rope. He said this was the only means of travelling in the outback. He has rented me the camel for five pounds, and said that no deposit was required as I reminded him of an uncle who once gave him a shilling. Then he drove us into town in his ute (a battered old pick-up truck) and showed us what we needed in the way of provisions. We bought:

Provision List

A camping table from the Grogman Camping Emporium
A book of stamps and twelve Kangermail envelopes
A map of Australia, detailed and illustrated
A Christmas cake
Dr Popper's Milky Bar Snacks x 12
Water bottles x 6
Three bales of hay
Porridge oats
Sardines
3 packets of long-grain rice
3 loaves of Easy-Slice bread
Margarine
12 apples
One jar of Vegemite (like Marmite, quite nice on toast)
6 tins of Good Dog dog food
A packet of Nutter's Aspirin for headaches
12 sausages
A camping stool
A washing line

This afternoon packed all our provisions, including the golf trolley, on to the camel. Roo has wasted some money on a silly plastic garden ornament, a rabbit holding a carrot. Will have to find room for it somewhere.

Shorty spent ten minutes with me, explaining how to make the camel do things like sit down and get up, and I think I picked it up quite quickly. I rode a horse when I was younger, and even a donkey at a fair, and it can't be too different. The camel makes the most disgusting noises, and is always belching. I have decided to call it Alf, though Roo thought Smelly would be a better name.

We do not need this plastic rabbit on the expedition!

Shorty gave me a wide-brimmed hat, called a drover's hat, with corks on strings to keep the flies away. He shook my hand and offered me five pounds and a week's free lodging at his shed in exchange for Roo. I told him that Roo was not for sale, not for all the money in the world.

I am going to send these letters now. Of course I will not be able to write to you when I am deep inside the bush, as there are no post offices. However, so that you can keep track of our progress, I shall keep a journal.

We have plenty of water. Bottles of the stuff! We will be all right.

with love Grandfather

Day 1

An excellent start to our journey. What a splendid idea to travel by camel. I am getting used to Alf's unusual gait, which is nothing like a horse's. Felt rather sick for the first few hours but feel much better now. However, my idea to attach Roo to the washing line so that she can track has not worked very well. She is supposed to run alongside Alf, as Shorty showed her, but she constantly forgets where she is going and often wanders off to look at things, causing many tangles. She will run neither behind nor in front of him but persists in running in and out of his legs, barking. Roo now rides on Alf too, as I wasted much time this morning getting her untangled.

We stopped for lunch under a blue gum tree, and there I studied the map properly for the first time. I calculated that if we rode steadily for a day or two we would definitely reach Gold Town. Shorty reckoned it would take us two days, so we should be there tomorrow evening.

Day 2

Tried to head north towards Gold Town as the map said, but it was impossible to keep to this route. Alf kept seeing interesting things to eat that lay in the opposite direction, and no matter how much I pulled on the reins, or kicked him with my heels, he paid no attention to me until his hunger was satisfied.

Made camp by a delightful pool that Alf chose. As I write this now, hordes of tiny insects are landing on my page, attracted by the light from my lantern, and I have to sweep the pages clear every minute to write.

We appear to be a little lost. Have not told Roo, as I don't want to start a panic.

Day 3
Gum Tree Junction

Something came into the tent last night, chewed a hole in my trousers and ate our Christmas cake. Unable to press on today, as Alf is unwell. He said he ate something last night and it has not agreed with him. Very cold today. Had to put on a pair of thick woolly trousers.

Alf with a case of the hump.

Day 4

It is raining very heavily. Where has the sun gone? Alf is in a foul mood. Threatening to go what he calls 'bad camel'. I do not like the sound of this at all. Can't seem to make out which way we are facing, as the compass appears to be broken. No sign of the sun to give us our bearings. The map is soaking wet and difficult to read in the rain. We are lost.

Day 5
Bongshang Valley

A lot more rain last night. Had to wear hat in bed as the tent is leaking. Filled a saucepan full of water beneath the hole. Roo lost plastic rabbit. I fear it has been swept away in the rain.

All around us tiny streams of water appeared from nowhere and I feared we would be washed away. The pool has risen higher. Must fix tent.

Roo said she was going home on the bridge back to England. I had to explain that there was no bridge and that we were on the other side of the world.

Though the rain pattering on the tent is a comforting sound, we do not sleep well. I seem to be lying on something very hard and lumpy, and my body feels every stone and bump beneath me. Roo very restless all night. Woke me up to tell me that my thick woollen trousers reminded her of an evil rabbit, with the buttons as eyes, and the trouser legs like ears. Had to get up and refold them, and when I had eventually got back into bed, with wet socks, she said that now they looked like a crocodile. Told her not to look at my trousers and to go to sleep.

Wish that Roo would sleep in her basket like a normal dog. Every time we pitch the tent she insists on dragging it inside, but then chooses to sleep in my sleeping-bag instead. Each time I put the basket outside she brings it back in again. There is little room enough in this tent. It is a 'one-man tent', not a 'one-man-and-his-dog-with-a-basket tent'.

Roo not getting up in the morning.

Day 6
Loud Belly Gorge

At last the rain has stopped.

Cooked large breakfast for Roo and me, and fed Alf some of the hay. Alf seemed a lot better this morning, though his temper has not improved. Packed all the equipment on to his back. It seemed lighter. I filled our empty water bottles at the pool.

We set off early in the morning. I was unable to ride on Alf, as he wouldn't kneel down to let me on. He said he had a sore hump. He and Roo do not get on well. Their constant bickering depresses me. It's always the same argument – who's the best, dogs or camels? Alf says that camels can store water in their humps and can live off their own supply of fat. Roo says that dogs live in houses and get fed, and don't need to store fat. Alf says that camels have special eyelashes to keep the sand out of their eyes. Roo says that dogs just shut their eyes and use their noses. And on and on, all day.

It feels very lonely out here in the bush. Of course Roo is good company, and so is Alf in a way, but I wish I had the company of humans occasionally.

Pitched tent beside a small stream where the ground was flat and soft. Gave Alf his dinner, then made Roo's. This caused another argument. However, at least we are comfortable. It is nice to have a table to write upon, something that I could never have carried had we not had Alf. Will go to sleep when I finish this.

Day 7

Another bad day! We only covered two or three miles today, as Alf said he felt a bit stiff. Also he complained that the camping table was rattling too much and made him nervous, so I had to leave it at a place called Pretty Sally's Hill. I hope she likes it. I did not see her. Roo said she was probably hiding behind a rock with her children.

Alf lay down and refused to get up, so I had to make camp as best I could on the spot that he had chosen, a miserable patch of scrubby grass beside a dead tree. Roo did not help me with the tent and said that instead she needed to hunt, as that is what tracker dogs do when they are resting. After I had finished pitching the tent she came running back in a very distressed state. She said she had been digging out a mouse from under a stone when a huge bear hanging upside down in a tree had jumped on her. She was reluctant to show me where the bear lived and, naturally, I was not keen to investigate. I didn't know they had bears in Australia.

Decided to build quite a large fire to keep the wild bears at bay. I have read that most wild animals are afraid of fire. You can pick up a flaming branch and just shake it at them and they will run away.

I tethered Alf to the dead tree and then I took guard with a golf club and a flaming branch. It began to rain again, and soon the ground was covered in large puddles and small streams began to form in the gully.

Roo was extremely alert, just like a proper tracker dog, keen to every minute sound. Her ears were like antennae, twitching and swivelling, and she barked at the smallest noise. Then I heard mewling in the bushes. It sounded like a lost kitten. Out of the clearing crawled a koala, no bigger than a teddy bear, and the little creature ran towards me with its tiny arms outstretched, almost as if I were its mother. The poor little thing was soaked to the skin and shivering miserably.

I wrapped it up in Roo's blanket and put it in my coat to keep warm. Then I carried it to the nearest eucalyptus tree, where I found its mother searching. How happy they were to see each other again. It was a wonderful little creature. I felt pleased to have done such a good deed, and could

even see the funny side of it.
Big bears don't pounce out
of trees on little dogs in
Australia. Had a good
laugh, I can tell you. Roo
embarrassed. Said it was
much bigger earlier and
must have shrunk in the
rain.

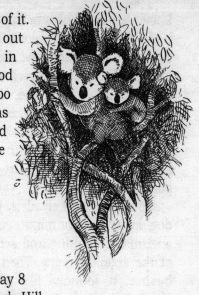

Day 8
Sprog's Hill

Today was a better day. We made excellent progress
up a hill and almost made it to the top, until Alf
decided he could go no further. We have camped by a
small cave in the side of the hill, just below the
summit. I pitched the tent, and built a small fire. I
put sausages on to grill and set a can on the embers,
just as Shorty had shown me back at Woolly Tree
Farm. As the light from our fire danced on the walls
of the cave I began to notice strange drawings
emerging through the gloom. Men and kangaroos
danced with wallabies and snakes. At first I thought
I was dreaming, for the figures and spirals seemed to
move in the light of the fire, and for a moment I was
sure that the kangaroos were hopping in a herd.

I took a burning branch, and by
its light I made out other
creatures in the painting –
strange birds and, best of all,
thought Roo, a huge sky rabbit. I
presume these must be the work
of the Aborigines.
They have lived in
Australia since the
beginning of time
and I have read that
nobody really knows
where they came from
before that.

Day 9

Although the compass now appears to be working I
am unable to get back on course for Gold Town.

The problem has been a combination of Roo, the
camel and other creatures. Alf has suddenly become
suspicious of large red boulders and won't go past
them. This has meant that we have had to press west
rather than east for most of the day. A gang of
kangaroos hopped right through our camp this
afternoon, breaking my teapot and knocking over a
bag of sugar, which caused an army of ants to rush
out of the long grass and attack us. Roo found a large
bone in the gully and wouldn't leave it alone. It was
too heavy for her to carry, let alone pick up, and so

she remained for an hour, hunched over it, growling like a wild beast whenever I tried to take it off her.

Quite lost this evening. Will we ever find Gold Town?

Day 10
Swagger's Creek

Alf took another large detour today, after he decided to follow a herd of wild camels. For the whole day he trudged after them, complaining and belching in the most horrible manner. I tried to tug at his head as Shorty had showed me, but nothing I did made him turn in the direction that I wanted him to go.

We trooped up several hills and descended a steep slope to a river, which on the map is called Swagger's Creek. It was good to see so much water, and I was relieved when the camels stopped to drink. I have read that camels can smell water and I was delighted to have witnessed a real demonstration of this feat. Roo said that she had smelt it too, several days before actually, but had forgotten to say so.

We made camp by the river.

I will not write much tonight, Child. The insects are in high spirits.

The wild camels are still with us, but the kangaroos have moved on, so it is peaceful.

The sound of the river running soothes me. I shall sleep well tonight.

Dreadful night. Woken by Alf with his head poking through our tent. Gave me quite a shock to open my eyes to that, I can tell you. Thought I was having a nightmare. His breath is foul in the morning! Alf said a monster had crawled out of the river and frightened all the camels away. He said he was unable to escape because I had chained him to a tree 'like bait on a hook', as he put it. He said the creature had a long neck and spines, and big round eyes like saucers. It only went away because my snoring scared it, said Alf. What nonsense!

Unfortunately this nonsense means that we can no longer follow the path by the river. Alf refuses to budge on this. Camels are very stubborn, as you know.

We are no nearer Gold Town. We might as well be back in England. Now we will never find Uncle Vincent.

Pressed on to try to find the route back towards Gold Town, but poor progress again today. Alf still following the herd of wild camels, which is not going the same way as we are. This is causing some friction between Alf and me. I had to show him who was the boss. Delayed giving him his dinner on time, which I think showed him who was in control.

Roo said that a lizard crept into my tent this evening and made off with one of my slippers. Asked her why she didn't stop it and she replied that it wasn't her job to guard slippers. Searched for slipper but no sign. What a nuisance!

Day 12

The wild camels have been following us all day. Made our camp beside a small stream while they watched from behind a bush. The leader of the pack, a large male with a big scar on his side, came over to Alf and tried to tempt him away from us. Said that he should be ashamed for allowing himself to be used as a beast of burden.

This has made things a lot harder for me, and although I fed Alf a loaf of our precious bread to prove to him that I bore no grudge, he still seems to be resentful towards me and has taken to calling me 'Boss' in a very sarcastic manner.

I hope that I don't have a camel mutiny on my hands.

A rare picture of Alf
Smiling. Probably because
he is eating. Typical!

45

Day 14
Lazy Bloke's Creek

Unable to travel for two days as the heat has been so unbearable. Yesterday it got so hot that even the wild animals became listless, and only the insects took delight in soaking up the full heat of the sun. We took shade in a pleasant grove of trees. Roo sat underneath a gum tree and chewed on one of my pencils. She says that she might write a book about rabbits for other dogs who might want to visit Australia. I said it was a very good idea, but, like a lot of Roo's ideas, I am sure that it will come to nothing. She lay under the tree for most of the day, only getting up to drink large amounts of our dwindling water supply.

Wild camels hanging around most of the day. Keep saying things to Alf that I can't hear and then all of them stare at me in a hateful way. Even Roo is in a bad mood with me, probably because she blames me for losing that plastic rabbit ages ago.

It really is quite useless. I have no idea where we are, let alone where your Uncle Vincent may be. Australia is a very big place, Child. It is easy to be daunted by its vastness. I feel like a needle in a haystack. Roo has not been the tracker dog that she promised to be. She does not get up early enough to be a real tracker dog. A real tracker dog would be up at the crack of dawn, eagerly sniffing at the trail. I am lucky if I can get Roo up at all, and when I have given her breakfast she often falls asleep. If I do get her going, she tends to track things that we are not looking for. Yesterday we spent a wasted afternoon in a dried-out creek, looking for something that Roo said was a clue. She sniffed around a scrubby bush and then began digging. After she had dug for ten minutes, she suddenly lost interest and found something more interesting in her tail.

How will we ever find Uncle Vincent with this attitude?

This evening I fed Alf the last of the hay and gave him a Vegemite sandwich as a sign of goodwill, but he just flung it over his shoulder and said he wasn't going to be bribed by a slave-driver. Left him sulking under a gum tree.

Day 15
Gormless Gulch

Alf has run away. I think he has gone off with the wild camels. He wasn't tethered last night because we had a row about me not trusting him. He said that he had his dignity and that real bushwhackers don't tether their camels and that he felt like a prisoner. In the end I felt so guilty that I left him untied. This morning he has gone, even taking one of my good blankets with him.

A Kookaburra.

Had to carry all our equipment now that Alf has gone, which meant leaving certain things behind. I decided that Roo's basket must go, as it has not been used once by her on the entire trip. She became very upset. She said I should leave her as well

48

if we couldn't take the basket. Had to take the wretched thing and leave some other useful things behind, like my camping stool, which I will miss in the evenings.

Day 16
Uncle Freddie's Pond

We have found the going a lot harder now that Alf is not here. Roo says it smells nicer, but I am afraid that without him we will not make much progress. Roo refuses to carry anything, as she says she is not a pack animal and is certainly not going to become a replacement for Alf.

Fortunately I have the golf trolley.

We crossed a series of small creeks, and I'm afraid that I had to carry Roo each time as she is certain that there are crocodiles in the water and doesn't want to get eaten by one. The bush became more arid and dry and I worried that we were going to enter a desert, although there is no mention of one on the map. Actually there are no names on the map for the bit that we are in at the moment, so I can't tell you where we are. Roo said that we could make the names up ourselves, so we did, and we named two trees after Roo and a dried-up pond after Uncle Freddie to make up for borrowing the golf trolley.

Pitched our tent by Uncle Freddie's Pond, as it is now known, and had a miserable dinner of sausages and porridge as we are running low on provisions.

Tidied up the tent this evening and tried to sort out our equipment. Found in the back of the tent a whole load of things that I don't remember packing. It seems that Roo has been dragging all sorts of things in here – bits of wood for gnawing on, a horrible old bone and a rancid old tin. Threw them all out,

watched by Roo in disgust.

She has become very despondent. First she says she wants to go home because she doesn't like Australia – her breed isn't suited to it. Although she said that her breed is expert on sand, she now remembers that it is soft grass that it is good on and not sand at all. Then she complained that the rabbits were too fast here and sometimes pretended to be stones, which wasn't fair. I gathered wood and pretended not to hear. I am far too concerned with our daily disasters to have to listen to this.

Day 17

Made our way today through a wide valley towards a big hill. Climbed all the way to the top, then found that there was an even bigger hill behind. Made camp on the top of the hill. Had to tie Roo to the golf trolley because I don't want any accidents.

What a nuisance! I wish Roo would not touch my ink bottle.

Later, when we were having our supper, an unruly gang of yelling kangaroos leapt through our camp, causing chaos. Pots and pans went flying and the guy ropes of the tent got tangled in their huge feet. They hopped away down the hill at great speed, dragging my tent behind them. Roo bolted after them, still attached to the golf trolley, which reared up behind her, scattering all our equipment and water bottles as she scrambled down the hill.

I set off after her, though it was difficult to keep up. We had soon covered quite a distance and I eventually found her barking into a small hole beneath a tree. She said they had all gone in there. It took me ages to drag her away from the hole, which wasn't big enough to hide a family of moles, let alone a herd of kangaroos.

At the bottom of a long gully lay the golf trolley. The frame was buckled and twisted. One of the wheels had snapped off and lay a few metres away. Further up the gully I found the tent hanging on a bush.

Now we were completely lost. Told Roo it was all her fault. She trotted off with her tail between her legs and said that she was going home, but she made sure that she was never out of my sight by pretending to find interesting things on the way.

I rescued the golf trolley, hastily packed it with as much of the equipment as I could find and folded the tent up. I stood on a rock and scanned the bush for signs of a landmark, but we were hopelessly lost. Our pots and pans were still in the camp back up the hill and would have to remain there. I hoped that maybe someone would find them and cook a meal in them.

The going was not easy with the one-wheeled trolley. I stumbled up the hill dragging the wretched thing behind me. Roo trotted ahead and pretended not to notice me. The ground was tough and dry. Large cracks in the soil formed nasty ruts that wore away at my ankles. I felt hot and angry. We climbed the hill for what seemed like a whole day. Then just as the sun was beginning to set, the top of the hill came in view. I staggered up the ridge and looked down to see an odd but welcome sight.

In a hollow depression sat a collection of houses clustered around a long, sloping, tin-roofed building,

lit with rows of coloured Christmas lights. There were balloons in the trees and scraps of coloured bunting draped across every house. Everywhere there were animals, of every description. Sheep and long-horned cattle milled up and down the main street. Mules and oxen strolled side by side through gangs of hopping kangaroos, and on the roof of every house large flocks of birds perched in long lines.

What luck! We have been saved. Went to look for help immediately. Could this be Gold Town?

Dear Child,

Great luck has befallen us. We have accidentally found Gold Town, a place that Uncle Vincent has mentioned many times in his postcards. He can't be too far away. The Gold Field is only five more miles from here, and as soon as the trolley is fixed we shall reach it in no time.

Our tent is pitched behind the pub in a field. It costs three dollars a night, four if you make use of the washing facilities — a tap and a drinking trough for horses. Grogman, the owner of the pub, said I could use any dunny* I found free, which I thanked him for. He said that Roo would have to use the field, which goes without saying. He watched as we pitched our tent as far away as possible from our only other neighbour in the field, a bad-tempered camel tethered to a post. I have decided I want nothing more to do with camels.

Gold Town is smaller than I thought it would be. It is not really a town at all, having only one street, Gold Street. There is a supermarket, a post office, a garage, a pub and a large barn called the Gold Town Home for Retired

* *toilet*

Pack Animals.

Went to the post office and was gladdened to find a parcel from you there. Thank you for the flip-flops. Although they are a size too big, they will be very useful for swatting flies with. Tell your mother that the shorts are an excellent fit and, despite the jeers I received this morning from some young kangaroos outside the post office, I will continue to wear them.

Unfortunately no news of Uncle Vincent. The man in the post office knows him but says he hasn't seen him for ages.

I have found a garage where I can get the golf

trolley fixed. It is a most unusual place, run by an old ram and a monkey. The monkey is incredibly fast at undoing nuts and bolts, because he can hold a spanner in each paw and one in his tail while working. They both stood around the broken trolley and shook their heads. Then at last the old ram sighed and said it would take a week to mend! He explained that he couldn't get the spare parts to fix the trolley.

The problem seems to be that here in Gold Town the kangaroos deliver all the letters, carrying the mail in their pouches. The drawback is that sometimes they get bored and post the letters in any old tree hole they can find, just to get the job done quicker. He said my order would be safe as it was going SPECIAL CLASS, which means a special class of kangaroo, I suppose. Anyway, must dash,

Hope this finds you well.

with love from
Your Grandfather

21 December
Gold Town

Dear Child,

Our second day in Gold Town. We went down to the garage to see how my trolley was getting on. Still in pieces. Went to the post office and got chatting to the mailing officer. It seems that Gold Town has seen better days. It was here that the miners flocked when the Gold Rush began. The town was full to the brim with them. The pub was filled night and day and there was a casino where everyone who had found gold could gamble it all

DO NOT ASK
FOR CREDIT
AS WE DON'T
HAVE ANY

away. When the gold ran out, the miners packed up and left. That's why there are so many animals here. They all used to work for the miners – pack mules and oxen for moving rocks, donkeys and camels for trekking, even canaries to go down the mines with the miners, and kangaroos for running errands and delivering mail.

We visited the supermarket and bought some more essentials. Roo wanted a bright red ball, which I bought for her, but I wouldn't allow her to spend her own money on a large inflatable Bugs Bunny. I explained that we didn't have room in the tent for Bugs Bunny.

I could see quite a few old mules hanging around outside the Gold Town Home for Retired Pack Animals as we went back to our tent. Bade them a good evening and they were most polite in their response.

Had a pleasant supper in the tent, with the lantern throwing a cheery light on us. Roo asked me to sing a Roo song.

It went like this:

I went looking for Wallamagoo,
I took a tracker and her name is Roo,
Yes, I have a dog and her name is Roo,
Bet you five dollars she's a good dog too!

61

I made up more of this nonsense – Roo loves it when I make the words only about her, and I have to try and sing as many verses of this as I can, making sure that they all rhyme, while she sits in her basket and smiles. I sang another twelve or so verses of this until she fell asleep.

She is sleeping quietly now at my feet, in her basket, where I hope she will remain. I am too tired to write any more, Child.

Goodnight.

with love,

Grandfather

P.S. These kangaroos are becoming a real nuisance. Yesterday I found a group of them rummaging around in our tent. One of the little ones had a pair of my underpants on!

22 December
Gold Town

Dear Child,

Trolley still not mended, as the old ram said that it had been in another accident. Wouldn't show me the trolley, which is very suspicious, but said that it would be ready on Christmas Day.

Another day wasted in Gold Town. We spent a lot of time keeping ourselves cool during the heat of the day, resting in the tent and reading the map. I had forgotten how noisy it could be in a tent. The fabric is so thin that you can hear a pin drop. Not only is there the non-stop chattering of insects, frogs and small birds to listen to, but this evening we had all the noise from the pub, plus the braying of Grogman's camel. Someone was playing a guitar badly and singing a rude song. Then a passable tune began, accompanied by much laughter, drumming on beer cans and the chorus of many kangaroos singing together. They were singing my Roo song but with different words. It went something like this.

An old man went looking for Wallamagoo,
Prodding with his stick his poor dog Roo,
Whacked his camel black and blue,
Watch it, mate, or he'll whack you!

Never have I prodded Roo and certainly I never laid a finger on Alf – or any other camel for that matter. I decided not to make a scene, but I shall complain to Mr Grogman when I see him for allowing such foul songs to be sung in his pub.

Decided that if we were going to be stuck in Gold Town for Christmas we would make the best of it. Of course we cannot prepare a huge Christmas dinner over our small camping stove, but we shall try our best. I have a surprise for Roo. Bought some Christmas decorations, some mince pies and a Christmas pudding. She has suddenly remembered it is Christmas and is very excited.

The sun was setting as we returned to our tent with the Christmas provisions. The pub was all lit up. An old oil-can was belching forth thick black smoke and I could smell bacon frying. Some dingoes slunk out of the trees and slipped into the pub. Roo began barking after they had gone inside, which brought out a few of the kangaroos to have a look. The kangaroos showed off, noisily jumping on to the tin roof of the pub and bouncing on it. Annoyed, I went to bed and put cotton wool in my ears to block out the sound of the raucous laughter and banshee wailing. At about midnight they stopped singing and then went home extremely quietly. I fell into a beautiful sleep.

Woke at three o'clock to the terrible sound of many trucks. It sounded as if we were going to be mown down. I struggled to get my clothes on, tripping over Roo, who was frantically trying to dig her way out of the tent, then opened the tent to an extraordinary sight. The whole of Grogman's was lit up, and the pub was surrounded by cars and trucks of every description. Possums were crammed into the backs of trucks driven by wombats, and everywhere were hundreds of sheep. Smaller creatures were there as well. The oxen and the water buffalo brayed madly as they jostled for spaces in the pub's car park. Then the music began and the animals made a dash for the huge pile of bottles.

They drank all night long. At one point a huge fight broke out among everyone — the duck-billed platypuses and the bandicoots excepted, for they are shy creatures and not prone to fighting.

This morning all is quiet. It is so hot that I cannot bear to stand in the sun. Roo lies panting under a tree. Only the kangaroos are still active, and were using my tent to jump over until I told them to stop it. Then they idled off, pausing nonchalantly to inspect a hole in a tree.

Put the rest of the decorations up to make our tent a little more cheerful. The kangaroos watched us all evening. Good supper of mashed potatoes and sausages.

Will send this letter to you in the morning as I expect we shall be on our way again soon.

with my love,
Grandfather.

Rat Kangaroos fighting over a tin.

The Christmas card that Grogman sent. Typical!

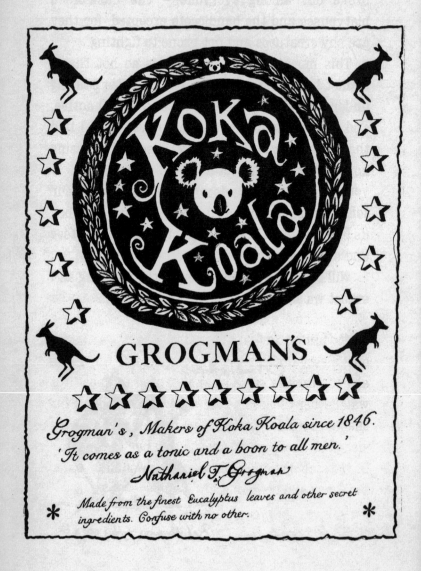

GROGMAN'S

Grogman's, Makers of Koka Koala since 1846.
'It comes as a tonic and a boon to all men.'
Nathaniel T. Grogman

Made from the finest Eucalyptus leaves and other secret
ingredients. Confuse with no other.

My dear Child,

A good day, spent making final preparations to get on the move again. I cleaned all our equipment. Roo said she couldn't see the point as it was bound to get dirty again. Ignored this.

The mules sent us a Christmas card, which was very nice of them, and I, in return, sent a box of toffees to their home.

Roo went to bed early to wait for Father Christmas. Eventually got to sleep around midnight, but woken at three o'clock in the morning by some of the kangaroos and three oxen singing Christmas carols outside our tent. Later a truck full of excited sheep drove past and yelled out 'Merry Christmas!' which woke Roo up. She is already excited enough, and wanted to know if it was Father Christmas arriving on his sledge. This then started her wondering how he would land his sledge if there was no snow. I told her that Father Christmas could land his sledge on sand or snow and he would be here soon, if she went to sleep.

with love from your Grandfather

Christmas Day
Gold Town

Dear Child,

An extraordinary thing has happened.

Woke on Christmas morning to the sound of complete silence. Struggled out of the tent to find that a thick carpet of snow had fallen in the night. Snow in Australia! How strange! Of course all the animals were completely stunned by the white stuff as they had never seen snow before. They didn't know what snow was. Even the kangaroos were quieter than usual and kept sniffing at it and jumping up and down on it.

Roo and I built a snow rabbit, and we soon had quite a crowd of animals watching us. I taught them how to do various different things with the snow. I showed them how to make a slide, which caused endless fun, especially for the kangaroos, who are very good at it. As you can see, their hind legs are perfect. I showed the animals how to roll the snow into balls, although I now regret teaching the kangaroos how to make snowballs. Massive snowball fight outside the pub and two windows broken. Took cover in our tent and unwrapped our presents. I got a pair of socks from your mother, a packet of jam labels from Roo, and an egg-timer from Uncle Freddie. I thought your present best though. I have always wanted a magnet set. Thank you.

Gave Roo her present. I admit that it is nothing exciting but our journey across Australia calls for practical measures. We cannot have the tent cluttered up with useless items, so I think my choice of a new dog collar was sensible. Quite annoyed to see it lying discarded behind the tent this afternoon.

The snow has already begun to melt as I write this. The animals are watching as it forms into puddles beneath a hot sun.

In the evening the old ram and the monkey, flanked by a gaggle of assorted creatures, wheeled my repaired golf trolley into our camp. There was much cheering as it was unveiled. Thanked the old ram and invited him to stay for Christmas dinner.

We shared out the mince pies and pudding, and soon many of the citizens of Gold Town came down to join us. The mules sang some very amusing Australian ballads that they had learned from the miners, and Roo particularly liked the one about a little dog and a tucker box. A possum sang a song about someone's roof he had lived in, which wasn't so interesting.

It was a most enjoyable evening, a good end to our stay in Gold Town. Tomorrow we will pack up and begin the final leg of our journey into Dust Valley.

Merry Christmas, Child.

all the best, your Grandfather.

Roo did
← this!

Dear Child,

Loaded the golf trolley and tied on as many water
bottles as we could. Water is most important to
us. Without it we would die in the desert. I have
decided to drag the trolley myself, as Roo says she
is too tired. Besides, she told me it is mostly my
stuff in it. We had an argument about this, and in
the end Roo said she would carry her own plastic
water bowl and nothing else.

The old ram and the monkey came to see us off.
We thanked them and I gave the old ram a woollen
hat, which I thought was silly afterwards, and
paid him for the repairs. Then we waved them
goodbye and began our journey to Dust Valley.

We looked back at the town only once, the silver
roof of Grogman's glinting in the sun. On the
horizon I could see the outline of the famous
Dangling Rock. It took us several hours to make
our way across the valley towards it. The sun was
relentless, and twice we stopped in the shade of a
blue gum tree. We were covered in a fine red dust,
and Roo looked like a little red dingo. Tied the
umbrella to her collar to give her shade while we

73

walked. The flies tormented us, buzzing around our heads in a thick black cloud. When we tried running to get rid of them they followed us.

We walked in silence for many miles, with only the sound of our feet crunching through the sand. We stopped for lunch beneath a tree. I shared out our water and was annoyed to find that Roo had dropped her water bowl and had to use mine. I don't mind sharing with a dog, but Roo asked if I could clean it after I had used it as she didn't want to catch any germs.

We will not walk in the heat of the day. As they say, only mad dogs and Englishmen go out in the midday sun, and we are not that foolish. I wrote a little and checked the map to see that we were still on the right course. On the horizon I could still see the outline of the Dangling Rock. So this time we must be heading in the right direction.

I can't write any more at the moment, Child. Roo has woken up and is running around in circles. She says she just got a whiff of something on the wind, perhaps Uncle Vincent's trail. We must be quick.

with love from your Grandfather
and Roo.

27 December
Near the Dangling Rock

Dearest Child,

What a nuisance! The scent that Roo picked up
was not Uncle Vincent's but a baby kangaroo's. We
found it hopping in tiny steps beneath the huge
Dangling Rock, calling for its mother. I picked it up
and put it in the golf trolley, which in a way is
quite similar to a mother kangaroo's pouch. It
seemed quite content with this and stopped
crying, but I am worried as we have no kangaroo
milk. An orphan is the last thing we need. It is

hard enough to look after ourselves, let alone an orphaned kangaroo. How will we feed it? I wanted to call it Little Roo, as it is less to say than Little Baby Kangaroo. Roo said she didn't want it called that, as she is the only Roo in the world and people would get confused. She suggested Ratty because, she said, it looked like one. Ratty is wholly inappropriate, so we settled on Joey, though I do not know if it is a boy or a girl.

Little Joey in his special pouch

Fed Joey with some crushed-up Milky Bar mixed with water. Used one of my socks to make a teat. Joey sucked hungrily. Roo sulked and said it was a waste of good chocolate.

There is nothing here to show that Uncle Vincent has ever been at the Dangling Rock. Perhaps I expected to find some writing on the rock to tell us that he had been here. But there is nothing, only the remains of a campfire, an old boot, and some strange marks in the sand.

After some tea and a sandwich, we

continued on our way. The ground had become very stony and it was hard going. I had to carry Roo most of the way as she said her paws hurt. This made the going even harder, what with Roo complaining that I wasn't carrying her properly. When at last I set her down to take a breather she shot off across the bush after something, scrambling into some prickly bushes. She came back half an hour later looking pleased with herself. I must say that I am heartily sick of the way Roo has behaved on this expedition. As far as she is concerned we are here only to go rabbiting. When I asked yesterday whom we were looking for, she said she had no idea what I was going on about, and she wanted to go home on the train. Although it pains me to hear her whining, we must press on and find my brother. I must be strong. I am the leader of this expedition, and weakness now would only ruin the progress we have made.

Ate supper in silence. Things moving in the long grass. Kept watch till midnight and built the fire up higher than normal to keep the things away. Roo slept in the bottom of my sleeping-bag as there was too much activity in the darkness. She lay there growling all night, which made it hard for me to sleep at all, and even when *I* moved, she barked. What with that and her claws poking into me, I hardly got a wink of sleep.

love Grandfather

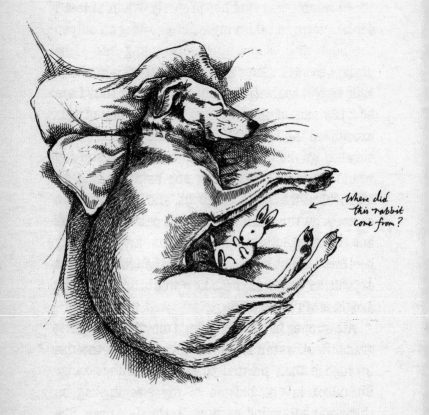

Where did this rabbit come from?

28 December

Dear Child,

Have been following a new trail that Roo found.
She was very excited, running around in circles.
She says she can smell an old man's footprints. I
asked her to tell me more, and she said she could
smell that the trail was recent, only a day or two
old. It must be Vincent. Who else would be out here
in this terrible place? Followed the new trail for a
whole day. You can imagine how I felt when Roo led
me into the old camp we had made last night.

Water is beginning to run low. We have enough
to last us a few days and no more. Took the last
bottle and placed it under a tree to keep cool. Ate
a meagre meal of sardines and spaghetti. Roo
finished off two plates and licked the saucepan
clean. I hate it when she does that, but I am too
tired to create a fuss.

Slept badly. Dingoes very restless.

with love, Grandfather

GOLD
FIELD

GOLD
TOWN

BROADWAY

Dear Child,   29 December

You can see that it is only a short distance from
Gold Town to the Gold Field. I am afraid that what
should have taken a day has taken three so far,
and we are still no nearer. This is because Roo has
led me on so many detours. What can I do when
my tracker dog hasn't got a clue?

Water is now down to the last cupful. I have
heard that the Aborigines can find water by
digging in the earth. Got a pickaxe and began to
dig. I dug for a while, and Roo joined in too before
she realized that we weren't digging for rabbits
and gave up. She sat and watched as I dug in the
blazing sun. I was giddy with the exertion of
digging. There wasn't even a drop of water to be
seen in the red dirt. The hole was now quite big,
almost deep enough to stand in. I took the pickaxe
and gave it one last swing, hitting something
hard. The next moment there was a huge gush of
water that knocked me off my feet and flew six
metres into the air, taking my hat with it.

We had struck water! What joy! Roo ran round
and round in circles, as she always does when she
is happy.

The water fountain never lessened its flow. We

81

were sprayed by the clear, cool liquid and stood underneath it as if it were a shower. We filled ourselves with as much as we could, drinking until we were full to bursting. Eventually the gushing dropped to a steady flow and the water formed a small pond. Flocks of budgerigars came to enjoy it.

About the middle of the afternoon we fell asleep under the shade of a gum tree. When we awoke we saw that the pond had now evaporated to a small puddle. We hastily filled our water bottles with as much water as we could carry, then left our little oasis behind and carried on further into the heart of the desert.

We soon came to a small huddle of tin-roofed shacks. An old man rushed out to see who we were. He seemed upset, and explained that he was waiting for the flying plumber because somehow his water pipes had burst and he had no water. I told him about the water we had found, showing him how I had dug the hole with the spade and pick and explaining about the shock I had had as the huge plume of water jetted into the air. I pointed to where the oasis was and offered to show him. Then for no apparent reason he became aggressive and belligerent. Why this valuable piece of natural

Roo did ← this!

82

survival information should anger him, I knew not, but I feared that he had been out in the sun too long and was suffering a type of sunstroke.

We left the old chap alone and headed towards a dirt track. Came across a rusty old sign proclaiming that this was the Gold Field. I had no idea that it would be so big. I suppose I had expected a small field with a fence around it. It wasn't so much a field as a country. It spread out for miles in front of us. We made poor progress across it. There wasn't much gold in sight for a place called the Gold Field, but everywhere we saw the remains of old shacks and deep holes in the ground where the miners had searched for gold

The heat is terrible. We have drunk a lot of water today.

Searched for Uncle Vincent all day – shouting his name until I became hoarse. But there wasn't another living soul in sight. What a lonely place this is!

Cannot write much more, Child. The insects are relentless in their attacks on my lantern, whole squadrons of them hurling themselves at the light. Roo and Joey are asleep. Do not worry about us, Child.

Your Grandfather.

30 December

Dear Child,

Still in the Gold Field. This part seems even more empty than the rest of the field and the ground is littered with small jagged rocks. Have not seen a mine or a shack for a long time now. It is hard to walk across the ground, so painful are these rocks. Had to put Roo in the golf trolley with Joey.

Camped by an old water tank. Tried to see if there was any water in it, but all that came out of the tap was some rust.

We are down to our last three bottles of water.

I feel very old tonight. Roo and Joey are asleep in my sleeping-bag. The evening's peace is broken only by the howl of the dingoes.

with love Grandfather

New Year's Eve
The Gold Field

Dear Child,

The sun got so hot today that the wheels of the golf trolley melted, leaving a black trail of melted rubber in our wake. We haven't seen another living thing, except for a couple of brown lizards, who seem well equipped to survive this terrible heat. The water is running low. We only have two bottles left. Made Joey some more milky, as he now calls it.

The situation is desperate, Child. The sun is getting hotter. There are no trees here and the only shade we could find was in a hole. I draped the tent over us to create some shade.

A hot wind blew all day long, and only in the

early evening could we begin our search again. When New Year came we held hands and I sang a bit from 'Auld Lang Syne', then drank some of the last of the water.

Down to our last water bottle.

with all my love,
Grandfather

New Year's Day
The Gold Field

Dear Child.

We drank the last drops of the water this morning.
Made Joey the last of the Milky Bar and water
mixture, but he cried for more soon after he had
been fed. I do not know what to do for the poor
little creature.

We have not moved today, as the sun is too hot.
Even the sand is sizzling gently.

with love Grandfather

Dear Child,

Too weak to dig for water. 'Water! Water! Water!' I found myself calling out this morning. Started off Joey, who cried for milky until his voice was just a squeak. Roo panting heavily. We are doomed to perish in this wretched place. What a fool I have been, bringing my dog to this desert.

I opened a tin of peaches and we all drank the juice greedily, but it only made us thirstier as it was full of sugar.

•

Water . . . Water . . . Splashing water, cool, cold waterfalls of water . . . Iced water . . . All we can think about. The sun shimmers in a giant heat haze. My mouth is parched and my tongue feels like I am sucking on a dry boot.

A little while ago I thought I saw a huge glass of water in the distance. Roo said she could see it too. Except it looked to her like a big red dog's bowl. We started to crawl towards it, dragging the trolley behind. Then it disappeared. Melted into the sand. It must have been a mirage.

•

If you ever get these letters, Child, you will see that Roo and I tried our best to find Uncle Vincent, but the desert made it impossible. I am sorry that we went away now. I can't bear to think that we will never see you again.

We are fading away, Child. It's all right. I am old. I have escaped death many times. But how I feel for Roo. What a brave dog she is.

Too weak to scrawl another line. I am thinking of you all. Tell your mother that I am sorry.

love Grandfather

9 January

Dear Child,

As we lay in that parched desert, the sun beating down on us relentlessly, I dreamed a dream. In the dream golden shafts of sunlight lit up a big black tunnel. Roo and I were floating down the tunnel towards the light. Then an old man with a big white beard appeared and took hold of us in his arms.

When we awoke we found ourselves in Uncle Vincent's shack.

He told us that he had found us when he was looking for his donkey, Eric, and would not have passed through that part of the Gold Field again for many months. I could hardly believe that the man who stood in front of me was Vincent. He looked so different. The last time I had seen him he was a young man. Now he was an old man. He told us that he had been searching for his donkey and had come across the three of us lying unconscious in the desert. It had been a big shock for him to discover that he had found his own brother.

I was too weak even to raise my head when he set water in front of me, but lapped at it off a plate. He fed little Joey two bottles of warm milk and gave Roo a towel soaked in water to suck on. Then he tucked all three of us up in his bed. I awoke several times, once to find the shack full of birds, with my brother feeding them birdseed.

Over the next few days, looked after by Uncle Vincent, we got our strength back. Soon Roo and little Joey were running around the shack, and I was able to sit up in bed and take in my surroundings. The shack was filled with Uncle Vincent's equipment. Spades and pickaxes, lanterns and prop shafts, bundles of rope and tins of dynamite – all the stuff that a gold miner needs to find gold. Except that Uncle Vincent

DANGER

hadn't found any. Now he lived here all alone, except for his donkey, Eric. Apart from the flying doctor he had no visitors, except the occasional flock of birds.

I am old, but I am happy, said Uncle Vincent. Today when we felt better he showed us the mine that he owned. We followed him up a small hill. In the side of the hill he had burrowed his way into the earth and rock, completing a huge tunnel into the hill. We did not go inside, for Uncle Vincent was afraid that the tunnel might collapse, as the timber props were now so old. Large piles of rocks were stacked in

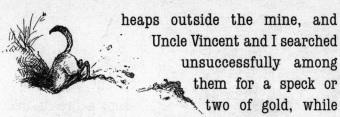

heaps outside the mine, and Uncle Vincent and I searched unsuccessfully among them for a speck or two of gold, while Roo dug away at an old rabbit hole in the side of the hill. Joey watched, fascinated, and even tried to join in until Roo told him off.

Uncle Vincent observed that Roo was an excellent digger and would have been very useful as a miner's dog. Roo told him, in between gnawing at a root that was blocking her way, that her breed is renowned as diggers and had even won cups for it. We watched as she dug deeper, until only the tip of her tail was showing, and then she disappeared into the hole. Joey hopped in after her and the two were gone.

They are still in the hole as I write this now. It is gone half-past nine, and though I have shouted down the hole most of the evening, they are still missing. Uncle Vincent shone a lantern down the rabbit hole, but all we could see was blackness.

*

93

All night we waited by the hole and kept a fire lit to watch it. It is now morning and there is still no sign of them. Roo was only showing off to Uncle Vincent, and has never been that far into a rabbit hole before. I put a plate of food by the hole so that she could smell her way back to us.

We sat by the hole all day, and Uncle Vincent tried to take my mind off Roo and Joey by telling me all the adventures that had befallen him in Australia. He told me about strange creatures that are so rare only the Aborigines have seen them – bunyips and bandicoots, giant kangaroos and huge lizards. He told me about the terrible snake creature that lives in the Snakey River, and I shuddered to think how close we had been to being eaten. Promised to apologize to Alf should I ever see him again.

Uncle Vincent's stories are quite fantastic, but

nothing could stop me thinking about Roo and little Joey. What if they had met a snake in the hole, or one of Uncle Vincent's horrible creatures?

Cannot write any more, Child. Uncle Vincent does not seem too concerned, and says they are both animals and will be fine. I am far more worried than he is, it seems.

with love,

Grandfather.

11 January
Uncle Vincent's mine

Dear Child,

This morning Roo and Joey were still missing. Sat sadly by the hole. How I missed my dog. I remembered the adventures we had shared. To have been cheated in the end by a stupid rabbit hole!

Then I heard a faint bark, and imagine my joy when out of the hole popped Roo's head, followed immediately by Joey! They were both covered from head to foot in a fine red dust, but apart from that they seemed fit and well, and even quite pleased with themselves.

So glad was I to see them that I immediately told them both off, but Roo jumped up into my arms and licked my face till it was wet. Then they went to their bowls and ate all their dinner.

When Roo had finished she sat on my coat and told us what had happened to them.

I listened incredulously as Roo described her

An artist's impression of the Rabbit King

journey down the hole, with Joey nodding in agreement behind her. How she had fought with a big rabbit in the darkness until she wrestled it to the floor, and how it had begged for its life and promised her a huge treasure in return. Roo had followed the rabbit (who, she added, was the King of the Rabbits) down the twisting tunnels into an enormous cave, where they stood surrounded by heaps of gold, which the Rabbit then kindly gave to Roo. Roo said she couldn't bring any of it out because she had no pockets and the smallest piece was too heavy to carry on account of its hugeness.

Then she added what I can only describe as a further ridiculous lie to this story, some nonsense about hundreds of rabbits coming out of all the other tunnels and bowing down to her, because she was the richest dog in the world.

I'm afraid I found this all too much to bear, what with the worry of losing Roo in the first place, and now this unbelievable story, and I was about to say so when Uncle Vincent, who had followed Roo's story with a very silly expression on his face, almost as if he believed it, jumped up and ran back to the shack. A moment later he reappeared, carrying spades and pickaxes, lanterns and rope. There was a wild look in his eyes.

He handed me a shovel and ordered me to dig.

It would have been useless to try and explain that this was just one of Roo's stories – he wouldn't have had it. Suffice to say we have not found a scrap of gold, just some old rabbit bones and a boot.

Must go. More digging to be done. What a waste of time!

All my love,
Grandfather.

Dear Child,

I know that this sounds like one of Roo's stories, but it is true. Uncle Vincent made the rabbit hole wide enough for him to crawl inside, and a moment later he was back, holding a large nugget of gold in his hand.

We have found gold! Enough gold to fill a barn. Roo ran round in circles, she was so happy, and I could only stand there blinded by the golden sheen. GOLD! GOLD! GOLD!

We loaded as much of the gold on to the donkey's back as he could manage, and filled the golf trolley. Then we trooped the short distance to Gold Town to celebrate our good fortune.

Tearful reunion between the kangaroos and little Joey. One of the large reds came and put his arm around me and thanked me for finding his son. The old ram and the mules drove us on the roof of a van round and round Gold Town to throngs of cheering animals.

Uncle Vincent bought the garage for the old ram and the monkey, and paid off all the other animals' rents on their homes and burrows as well. He ordered several sofas so that the pack animals in the retirement home would be more comfortable. He bought Grogman's pub and gave out free cans of Koka Koala till stocks ran dry. Sent Grogman cheerfully on his way with a piece of gold the size of a walnut. Grogman loaded all his stuff on to his camel and sneaked off. Then Uncle Vincent opened the supermarket and gave out wheelbarrow-sized loads of food to all the citizens of Gold Town. Some koala bears were so laden down with leaves that they could hardly walk.

Kangaroos, freed from their duties as postmen, thronged about us in the streets and tied eucalyptus leaves about our brows.

Roo was carried on the back of an ox through crowds of cheering possums and wombats. Uncle Vincent organized a cricket match against the kangaroos, but they won by a century. After the match Uncle Vincent took my hand and squeezed

it. He never usually does that sort of thing, and, being a man of few words, he told me bluntly that he was glad I had come to find him, but he had never been lost in the first place. Then he said that it wasn't the finding of the gold that was the important bit, it was the looking. Australia was his home and he could never bear to be in another part of the world. Roo agreed and said it was the same with rabbits. Uncle Vincent said he wanted to stay and look after Gold Town and the surrounding bush till he died. He said he would spend his share of the gold on keeping it wild. This would make him happiest.

And so we hugged Uncle Vincent and little Joey goodbye and this morning we left on the bus to Sidney. They waved us all the way out of Gold Town until they were soon just tiny specks in the distance.

As I write this down, Child, we are high up in the air in a plane on our way home. I miss Uncle Vincent and so does Roo. But I promised that we would come back next year. Next time you can come too.

We are travelling first class in a brand-new plane. Roo has just been to see the pilot to ask if she can have a go at steering it. I'm sure he will agree.

After all, it is Roo's plane.